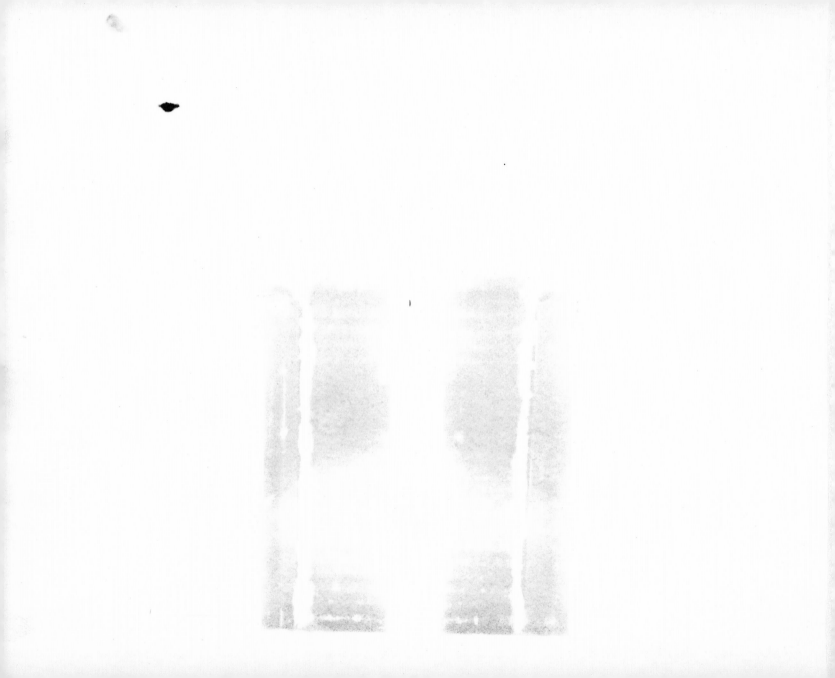

Jam
FOR
Nana

THIS BOOK BELONGS TO

_____

_____

A Random House book
Published by Random House Australia Pty Ltd
Level 3, 100 Pacific Highway, North Sydney NSW 2060
www.randomhouse.com.au

First published by Random House Australia in 2014

Addresses for companies within the Random House Group can be found at
www.randomhouse.com.au/offices.

National Library of Australia
Cataloguing-in-Publication Entry

Author: Kelly, Deborah, author.
Title: Jam for Nana / Deborah Kelly; illustrated by Lisa Stewart.
ISBN: 9780857980014 (hardback)
Target Audience: For pre-school age.
Subjects: Grandparent and child--Juvenile fiction.
Other Authors/Contributors: Stewart, Lisa, illustrator.
Dewey Number: A823.4

Cover and internal design by Alicia Freile/Tango Media
Printed and bound in China by Midas Printing International Limited

Jam
FOR
Nana

Deborah Kelly · Illustrated by Lisa Stewart

When Nana makes pancakes, I spread the jam.

I smooth it right to the edges with the back of
my spoon, until it looks like a giant orange sun.

Then we roll them up tightly, dust them with
sugar and lick our fingers.

Nana waves her spoon.

This isn't jam. Not real jam. Real jam tastes like the sun.

She shakes a great dollop onto another pancake.

How many apricots do you see?

I shrug.

Nana turns her spoon upside down. The jam slides off.

Uh-oh! See? Not real jam.

I lick the spoon and my sticky fingers.

Did you have real jam when you were little, Nana?

In the old country we had apricot jam with
the warmth of a hundred summers. You could
count the apricots. You could hold the spoon
upside down and shake it.

I want real jam, Nana! Let's go and get
some – together!

Nana shakes her head.
It is too far.

Is it too far to walk?

Yes.

What if I took my scooter?

Too far, even for that.

What if I had an aeroplane?

Or a really big boat?

Then we could fly high above the
clouds, or sail across a great ocean,
like I did when I was a girl.

I want Nana to have *real* jam again.
Maybe I can find another way to make her
feel the warmth of a hundred summers.

When I'm finished, I ask Nana if we can
make more pancakes.

We spread the jam right to the edges,
with the back of a spoon.

We roll them up tightly, dust them
with sugar and lick our fingers.

Together, we taste the sun.

My darling, Nana whispers as she cuddles
me tight.

This, now this, is real jam.